Dinner Ladies Don't Count

Dinner Ladies Don't Count

Bernard Ashley

Illustrated by Janet Duchesne

Julia MacRae Books
A division of Franklin Watts

Text © 1981 Bernard Ashley
Illustrations © 1981 Janet Duchesne
All rights reserved
First published in Great Britain 1981 by
Julia MacRae Books
A division of Franklin Watts Ltd.
12a Golden Square, London W1R 4BA
and Franklin Watts Inc.
387 Park Avenue South, New York 10016

Reprinted 1982, 1983

British Library Cataloguing in Publication Data
Ashley, Bernard
    Dinner ladies don't count. – (Blackbirds).
    I. Title   II. Series
    823'.9'1J   PZ7.A8262
ISBN 0-86203-017-X UK edition
ISBN 0-531-04281-2 US edition
Library of Congress Catalog Card No: 80-83008

Made and printed in Great Britain by
Camelot Press, Southampton

Chapter 1

Jason Paris stormed along Sutton Street. He pulled a fierce face at three girls strung across the pavement and turned left into the school playground. Inside, he kicked every plank in the fence and threw a stone at the huge rubbish bin. It clanged a warning to everyone. Jason had come to school with a smack instead of breakfast and they

were all likely to feel the sting.

He barged backwards into the classroom. Miss Smith stopped smiling at Donna Paget's birthday cards. There they were, all love and kisses in her hands—but there was Jason knocking into chairs. There was a time and a place for everything, and she had to stop someone getting hurt.

"Hello, Jason. Do you want to use the plasticine this morning?" she asked. Miss Smith knew the look, knew the sound of trouble.

"No!" Jason dug his hands into his pockets and glared at anyone foolish enough to look at him.

Donna Paget scooped up her birthday cards and pushed them hurriedly into her tray. "He spoils everything," she said.

"Would you like to read a book?"
Miss Smith was asking.

Growling something in his throat,
Jason cut a path through chairs
and children to the book corner. He
kicked a cushion and threw himself
to the floor with a book. He could
smell the dust in the hard, thin
carpet. He felt the rough ridges
beneath his elbows. It was a cheat,
the book corner, he thought. It
looked nice, but the floor and the
books were too hard. He'd like to
throw the books all round the room.

The book he had was big and
flat and had sharp corners. It
would be a good weapon. He stared
at the shiny cover. All about dogs.

Dogs! It would be about dogs! He twisted it in his hands like a bar bender in a circus, hoping it would bend and crack. But it was tougher than he was. Red in the face, he had to give up.

He stared at the poodle on the
cover and he thought about his dog,
Digger. Digger, small and tough,
that got through little cracks and
came back with bones. Digger,
that let only him put his lead on,
that trotted by his side and looked
up when he talked to him.

Digger, that waited for him while
he did things, that barked at people
he wanted to frighten, and bit people
he wanted bitten. That was his
dog, Digger.

Poor Digger. Jason's stomach
rolled with an empty feeling of loss.
He felt sad—and to think that on
top of that he'd had a hard smack,
just for making a fuss about it!

Miss Smith didn't bother Jason with Maths but it was a lot of cutting out paper shapes: squares, triangles and circles. The gummed colours were stuck into Maths books, and the bits left over went into the bin. Everyone else was doing it.

With one half-closed eye Jason watched the activity, all the moving about for fresh colours, all the trips to the bin with the scraps. He watched and he waited until Donna Paget was up at the desk, part of a soft wall of good girls, hiding him from view.

Chapter 2

Donna's plasticine model of the
Red Pirate was on a piece of board
standing on the window sill. It
wasn't far away. It took only a few
seconds to walk over to it and press
it down flat with the book about
dogs. Jason pulled the book off with
a tacky jerk and slid back to the
book corner. Served her right for
showing off about her birthday,

he thought. Now the Red Pirate
was a red dwarf. And serve the
book right, too. The stupid poodle
deserved to have plasticine on it.

Jason waited: and just as if he'd
lit a fuse it was only a few moments
before the explosion. Tears and
shouts littered the room like the
paper. Everyone was sent to their
places while Miss Smith stood over
the squashed model. Donna sobbed,
blotchy and red, while the girls on
her table crowded to comfort her.

"What a terrible thing for anyone to do! This was no accident. Some little hooligan has done this!" Miss Smith said.

"If you cry on your birthday you cry all the year," said Jason.

Miss Smith looked at him. "Jason Paris, let me see your hands." She was over to him in the two strides it had taken him to get to the model. He put them out, grubby, but free from plasticine. He had thrown the book down to give them to her, though, and the wrong side had landed up.

"Worse than I thought!" Miss Smith said. "You've ruined a good book to do it!" She was really angry.

The room went silent. Donna's tears had dried, her eyes had narrowed. Everyone was waiting to see what would happen next. Squares, triangles and circles gummed themselves to the wrong places while they held their breath and watched.

"You're a nasty, naughty, little boy, and none of us wants you in our room, do we, children?"

"No!" they chorussed, looking at one another with good faces.

But suddenly Miss Smith seemed

to turn into someone else. She
crouched down to Jason's level and
held him by the shoulders. "Oh,
Jason! Why, love?" she asked,
softly.

No-one heard any answer.
Donna started crying again and
the rest chattered in their mixed-up
disappointment. It looked as if he
wasn't going to be put out of the
classroom, or taken to Mrs. Cheff,
after all.

It was left there, in the air. Mr.
Lee, the caretaker, came in to
change the roller towel and he saw
the overflowing bin. He tut-tutted
at the mess and took it out to empty:
and that filled the last few minutes
before play.

14

During play-time they talked,
Jason and Miss Smith. She drove
the others out and took him to her
chair, where she spoke in a quiet
voice and tried to look him in the
eye.

"You came in this morning like a
bear with a sore head," she said.
"Did you get out of the wrong side
of the bed?"

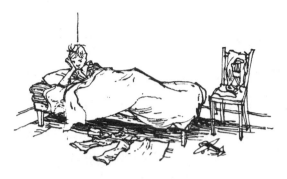

Jason frowned. When your bed
was against the wall there was
only one side you could get out.
And what did getting out of bed
have to do with any stupid bear?
He didn't see what she was getting
at. It was his dog, Digger, he'd
been thinking about when he got
out of bed.

"You think about it while I run and get my tea," Miss Smith said. But it didn't get them anywhere. When she got back, Jason could still only stare silently at the floor.

They were frozen like that, in failure, when the others came in from play. "You'd better sit down, Jason," Miss Smith said, "and be nice and good for the rest of the day."

Jason didn't know whether he would or not. He didn't feel like being bad any more, and yet he didn't feel like being good. But he definitely wasn't ready to be *nice*. Just to be left to himself to get over Digger seemed about right for him.

"Come on, it's time for P.E. in the hall. A run round will do you good."

He had just got his shorts from his tray when a new shriek from Donna made every back in the room go rigid.

Chapter 3

"They're gone!" she screamed,
staring with bolt eyes at Miss
Smith. Her fists were clenched and
her pink arms were shaking. "My
birthday cards! Out of my tray!"

Her tray was on the table.
Already, friendly hands were
searching in it, checking in case the
cards were in her books: and while
the shrieking went on the undressed

room looked in the other trays, in
vases, in the fish tank, even.

But Miss Smith was looking in just one place—at Jason. Slowly, she crooked her finger and drew him to her. He went, willing and innocent. After all, he hadn't taken Donna's cards, had he?

"I'm going to give you just ten seconds to tell me where they are. I tried to help you. I trusted you. I left you on your own while I went to get my tea, and you repaid me by doing something stupid with Donna's cards. Now, where are they, before I get really cross?"

"I don't know, Miss. Honest!"

"One, two, three, four . . . You're a very unkind boy. Five. I don't like people who *won't* be helped.

Six, seven, eight, nine, ten."

She seemed to speed up at the end. There was no nine-and-a-half, no nine-and-three-quarters this time. She wasn't bluffing. She was ready to do what she'd threatened before.

"Come on, to Mrs. Cheff. And the rest of you get changed back. We've missed our hall time now, thanks to one of us. . . ."

Miss Smith led Jason by the wrist along the corridor to the head's office.

Mrs. Cheff's door was open. Jason could see her in there, getting the birthday log ready with the candles on it. A birthday badge lay like a medal on the table. It would be his turn next week, but he didn't want it to come any more.

Soon Mrs. Cheff had him on her own. "Well, Jason, this is all very disappointing. Now what would possess you to do a thing like this? Why are you in such an ill humour?"

Jason looked at Mrs. Cheff's shoes. He wasn't ill, or funny or anything. Everything would be all right if he hadn't had the bad news about his dog, Digger.

And he no more wanted to touch Donna Paget's cards than he wanted one of those birthday badges for himself next week.

There was a knock at Mrs. Cheff's door. She had a lot to do.

"Well, I'm going to give you till the end of dinner time to find them," she said. "Or I'm going to have to write a letter home. You can look through the book corner and see if they haven't got tucked inside a book . . ." She gave him a knowing look. She knew where boys hid things like other people's birthday cards, it said.

Mr. Lee came in with some letters. He slid them round the door so as not to disturb her. Mr. Lee had a tattoo on his arm which Jason admired: a tiger's head with bared fangs. Jason always looked for it.

Suddenly, seeing it now, he remembered that he'd seen it once before that morning. Yes! When Mr. Lee had emptied the bin of paper . . .

Now he knew where to look for those cards. He didn't understand what Miss Smith and Mrs. Cheff went on about half the time; but now he did know how he could stop himself getting another smack at home.

Chapter 4

The huge rubbish bin was chained
to the fence in the playground.
Every Monday morning the rubbish
lorry came and picked it up like
some robot drinking from a giant
mug. You could get up on the bin,
if you used the chains for your feet,
and then you could look down
inside. It was very dangerous, and
against the school rules. On the
other hand, Jason knew where the

birthday cards were—and at dinner
time there were only dinner ladies
on duty.

As soon as the rest went into the
kitchen he ran to the bin. He
jumped for the chain and started
hauling himself up the cold, smooth
side.

"Here, you're not supposed to go
up there," a big girl told him.

"Don't care. Mind your own business."

"Mrs. Moors can see you."

"Clear off!" He reached for the rim.

"She's a dinner lady. You'll get into trouble."

"Dinner ladies don't count," he said, and he heaved himself on to the flat top. Now all he had to do was take the small lid off and look down inside. Being Friday, this morning's rubbish shouldn't be hard to reach.

But Mrs. Moors came quicker than the lid came away in his hand.

"Jason, get down from up there," she said. "You'll fall down inside."

He didn't reply. He tugged at
the rubbery lid, and at last it came
away, heavy in his hand.

"I said, come down!"

"I'm looking for something."

"What are you looking for?"

"Something."

He didn't like the smell coming
up; and it was darker in there than
he'd thought. But the real trouble
was, he couldn't reach the top

layer of rubbish, not without climbing in. He looked down outside for Mrs. Moors again: could he get in before she stopped him? But she wasn't where she had been, beside the bin. She was coming across the playground, carrying a pair of steps.

If she was coming up to drag him down he'd have to get in quick!

"You get in there and I'll kill you!" she shouted. "Never mind what Mrs. Cheff says."

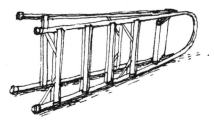

It stopped Jason dead.

"Now let's see what you're so blessed worked up about. A ball, is it?" Mrs. Moors was up the steps and reaching down into the bin. She scooped up handfuls of coloured paper. "No ball in here," she said.

"It's birthday cards. Someone's thrown out Donna Paget's birthday cards, and I've got the blame."

Mrs. Moors went on scooping. "Well, you can't blame them for that," she said. "You've had the hump all day, haven't you? I saw you pass my window this morning, all in your temper." She took out grabs of paper and let them drift back down. "There's no cards in

here, Jason." She put the lid back.
"Now, you come down and tell me
what's given you the hump."

Jason came down. He liked this
dinner lady. He understood her.
She seemed to talk the same way
as he did. Yes, he'd had the hump
all right, been in his temper. But
it wasn't his fault, was it, after
what had happened?

Chapter 5

He told her, there behind the bin.
He thought she'd understand.

"It's my dog," he said. "Digger.
He's not really a dog yet, he's one I
was going to have next week. For
my birthday. My mum promised
me years ago. But now she says
she's made ill by dog's fur, and I
can't have one." He kicked the
fence again, remembering.

"Oh." Mrs. Moors seemed lost for a word. "Allergic," she said, after a few seconds. "Gets up her nose, I suppose."

"Yeah, and she gets up mine!"

Mrs. Moors laughed, and ruffled his hair. "Oh, come on, she has a lot to put up with, your mum. She's probably thinking it wouldn't be fair to the dog, her out to work all day, the dog cooped up."

Jason kicked the fence again.

"Hard old life, isn't it, Jason? I wish I had a dog you could walk for me—but I haven't. You've just got to swallow it, wait till your mum's ready. It'll happen one day, you see . . ."

Jason shrugged. Who knew when that would ever be? And in the meantime he was still in trouble over Donna Paget's birthday cards. "The cards," he said. "I know I never went near them."

"Well, they're not in the bin, so they're somewhere in your classroom," Mrs. Moors said. "Come on, let's turn it upside down."

Miss Smith was in the classroom, carefully stretching the Red Pirate to something like his right size. Mrs. Moors went over to her and they had a very quiet conversation. Jason knew what it was about. Mrs. Moors was telling Miss Smith about his birthday, and Digger.

While they talked Jason thought back to that morning. In his mind he came into the classroom again, and he tried to see what he'd seen before. He saw Donna Paget grabbing up her cards and pushing them into her tray. She'd done it all in a rush, as if he was going to tear them up.

Jason went over to the tray unit.
Donna's tray was at the top, with
her name on it. He pulled it out. As
usual on P.E. days, it was stuffed
full with plimsolls and a tee-shirt.
It was chock-a-block, like his own
untidy drawers at home.

And then he knew where to look:
where he sometimes found things
if he turned his own room upside
down, like Mrs. Moors had said.
Where his football programmes
went if he over-stuffed his drawers.
Down the back, where top things

slid if you pulled the drawer in and
out carelessly.

Sure enough, there they were:
all the cards, chewed and bent at
the back.

"Look!" he said. But he didn't
touch them. He didn't want
anyone to think he'd put them back.

"Oh, lovely. Well done, Jason.
How clever! You see?"

The two women were beaming: and inside Jason felt pleased.

Miss Smith turned to Mrs. Moors. "I was mistaken," she said. "Because he was naughty once I blamed him twice. Give a dog a bad name!"

Jason frowned. Now he didn't understand again. Was she talking about him? She had to be, he thought, because Digger was a *good* name to give a dog.

And one day he'd give a dog that name; when the time came . . .